Dear Parent:

Congratulations! Your child is taking the first steps on an exciting journey. The destination? Independent reading!

STEP INTO READING® will help your child get there. The program offers five steps to reading success. Each step includes fun stories and colorful art. There are also Step into Reading Sticker Books, Step into Reading Math Readers, Step into Reading Phonics Readers, Step into Reading Write-In Readers, and Step into Reading Phonics Boxed Sets—a complete literacy program with something to interest every child.

Learning to Read, Step by Step!

Ready to Read   Preschool–Kindergarten
• big type and easy words • rhyme and rhythm • picture clues
For children who know the alphabet and are eager to begin reading.

Reading with Help   Preschool–Grade 1
• basic vocabulary • short sentences • simple stories
For children who recognize familiar words and sound out new words with help.

Reading on Your Own   Grades 1–3
• engaging characters • easy-to-follow plots • popular topics
For children who are ready to read on their own.

Reading Paragraphs   Grades 2–3
• challenging vocabulary • short paragraphs • exciting stories
For newly independent readers who read simple sentences with confidence.

Ready for Chapters   Grades 2–4
• chapters • longer paragraphs • full-color art
For children who want to take the plunge into chapter books but still like colorful pictures.

STEP INTO READING® is designed to give every child a successful reading experience. The grade levels are only guides. Children can progress through the steps at their own speed, developing confidence in their reading, no matter what their grade.

Remember, a lifetime love of reading starts with a single step!

For Lucy Rae
—M.L.

Visit us on the Web!
StepIntoReading.com
www.randomhouse.com/kids

Educators and librarians, for a variety of teaching tools, visit us at
www.randomhouse.com/teachers

Library of Congress Cataloging-in-Publication Data
Lagonegro, Melissa.
Beautiful brides / by Melissa Lagonegro ; illustrated by Elisa Marrucchi.
p. cm. — (Step into reading. Step 2)
ISBN 978-0-7364-2685-5 (trade) — ISBN 978-0-7364-8087-1 (lib. bdg.)
I. Marrucchi, Elisa. II. Title.
PZ7.L14317Be 2010 [E]—dc22 2009042731

Printed in the United States of America   10 9 8 7 6 5 4 3 2 1

DISNEY PRINCESS

Beautiful Brides

By Melissa Lagonegro

Illustrated by Elisa Marrucchi

Random House 🏠 New York

Belle is going
to marry the Prince.
She loves her
wedding gown.

She wants to plan
the perfect wedding.
There is a lot to do!

Belle makes
a guest list.
She invites
all her friends.

Belle tries wedding cakes.

They taste so good!

She picks out

the best one.

Belle's wedding day
is here!
Her father walks her
down the aisle.

The Prince sees
his beautiful bride.
Belle and the Prince
say "I do!"

Aurora will be
a lovely bride.
The good fairies help
her choose a gown.

Which one will she pick?
They are all so pretty!

Aurora and Phillip
are husband and wife.
They have a big party
to celebrate!

Aurora tosses
her flowers
to her friends.
Who will catch them?

Ariel's wedding day
is here!
She brushes her hair.
Sebastian helps her
with her veil.

Ariel and Eric
take their vows.
They are married at last!

Ariel and Eric dance
their first dance.
Sebastian sings.

Ariel's family watches
from the sea.
King Triton is
very proud.

It is Snow White's
wedding day.

Her animal friends
help her get ready
to marry the Prince.

The Dwarfs make
Snow White
a wedding gift.
It is a fancy crown
and a necklace.

Snow White is
a perfect bride!

Cinderella puts on
her wedding gown.
It is long and white.

The Fairy Godmother
uses her magic.
The gown sparkles!

Cinderella and the Prince
take their vows.
The Prince gives
Cinderella
a wedding ring.

The bride and groom ride
into the sunset.

They are so happy!

Jasmine is almost ready
for her wedding.
She chooses the
perfect flowers.

They look lovely
with her gown!

The palace is filled
with guests.
Aladdin smiles
at his bride.

This is the happiest day
of their lives.

Tiana and Naveen
are married!
They share a kiss
as husband and wife.

Their friends
clap and cheer.

It is a wonderful day!

Tiana and Naveen
are in love.
They live happily
ever after.